The
Poet's Dog

The Poet's Dog

PATRICIA MacLACHLAN

KATHERINE TEGEN BOOKS
An Imprint of HarperCollins Publishers

Katherine Tegen Books is an imprint of HarperCollins Publishers.

The Poet's Dog
Text copyright © 2016 by Patricia MacLachlan
Illustrations copyright © 2016 by Kenard Pak
All rights reserved. Printed in the United States of America.
No part of this book may be used or reproduced in any manner whatsoever without
written permission except in the case of brief quotations embodied in critical
articles and reviews. For information address HarperCollins Children's Books, a
division of HarperCollins Publishers, 195 Broadway, New York, NY 10007.
www.harpercollinschildrens.com

ISBN 978-0-06-229262-9 (trade bdg.) — ISBN 978-0-06-229263-6 (lib. bdg.)

Typography by Ellice M. Lee
16 17 18 19 20   PC/RRDC   10 9 8 7 6 5 4 3 2 1
❖
First Edition

THIS BOOK IS FOR
EMILY—

WITH LOVE,
P. M.

Dogs speak words
But only poets
And children
Hear

—P. M.

CHAPTER ONE

Lost and Found

I found the boy at dusk.

The blizzard was fierce, and it would soon be dark.

I could barely see him with the snow blowing sideways. He stood at the edge of the icy pond, shivering.

He had no hat, and his blond hair was

plastered to his head.

Suddenly a limb cracked and fell down next to him, and when he jumped to one side, he saw me coming through the drifts of snow toward him.

I nosed his hand gently. He wasn't afraid of me.

He was afraid of the storm. I could see tear streaks on his face.

He led me to his sister crouched under a big tree, a blanket wrapped around her. She was younger, maybe eight. The boy pulled the blanket more tightly around her.

I nosed her, too. When she stood up, my eyes looked into hers.

I would take care of them.

I'm a dog. I should tell you that right away. But I grew up with words. A poet named Sylvan found me at the shelter and took me home. He laid down a red rug for me by the fire, and I grew up to the clicking of his keyboard as he wrote.

He wrote all day. And he read to me. He read Yeats and Shakespeare, James Joyce, Wordsworth, Natalie Babbitt, and Billy Collins. He read me *Charlotte's Web*, *The Lion, the Witch and the Wardrobe*, *Morning Girl*, and my favorite story, *Ox-Cart Man*. So I saw how words follow one another and felt the comfort of them.

I understand words, but there are only two who understand me when I speak.

Sylvan once told me this.

"Poets and children," said Sylvan. "We are the same really. When you can't find a poet, find a child. Remember that."

Remember that.

The boy held on to my body to help him stand in the wind.

"Help," he said.

I knew what his word meant.

Sylvan taught me about rescue.

I would save them the way Sylvan had saved me.

The boy took his sister's hand, and they followed me. We hurried through the woods, past the big rock, down the path by the shed where I had slept after Sylvan was gone. It had only been three days. I had learned to count:

Day and night one.

Day and night two.

Day and night three.

Or was it four days? Being alone confuses the truth about time.

Sylvan's poetry students took turns feeding me. Ellie, my favorite, knew that I couldn't sleep in the house with Sylvan gone. She would have taken me home with her, but she knew I couldn't leave either.

The boy put his hand on my neck. It felt good to me. Sylvan used to walk in the

woods with his hand on my neck. Sometimes he spoke in poems.

I felt like crying. But here's another
truth: dogs can't cry. We can feel sadness
and grief.

But we can't cry.

"Where are we going?" the girl asked,
her clear voice like a bell. The wind
whipped her hair across her face.

"Home," I said, speaking for the first
time.

She wasn't surprised I spoke.

She put her face close to my ear so I
could feel her warm breath.

"Thank you," she whispered.

I wished I could cry.

CHAPTER TWO

Home

We reached the clearing, struggling through the snow and wind.

"Oh!" said the girl when she saw the cabin.

There was the light in the window. Sylvan had kept it on all the nights and days we lived together.

"It's our beacon," he'd told me.

I knew the door wouldn't be locked. I nosed the lever on the door open. Sylvan had given me the lever so that I could go in and out as I wanted.

We stepped out of the howling of wind into the quiet.

The boy and girl stripped off their coats and I shook snow from my fur.

"I'm Flora," said the girl. "I'm cold. My blanket is wet. He's Nickel," she added, pointing to her brother.

"I'm Nicholas," he said. "Flora calls me Nickel."

"I'm Teddy," I said. "I like Nickel."

It was dark except for the one beacon

light. Nickel turned on two lamps.

"Can you build a fire?" I asked him. "There's wood and kindling on the hearth."

He nodded.

"I'm almost twelve."

Flora hung up her coat on a hook by the door.

"Why are you lost?" I asked.

"The car slid into a snowbank, and my mother couldn't get it started again," said Flora.

Nickel had stacked kindling and wood in the fireplace. He found the matches on the mantel.

"She left her cell phone at home. She saw the lights of a house down the road where a family had been shoveling and left us to get help," he said.

"She was gone a long time," said Flora.

"We could have stayed in the car, but people came and knocked on the car windows, telling us the car was going to be towed off the road before it got covered with snow," said Nickel. "Flora was scared."

"Nickel was scared, too," said Flora, making Nickel smile.

Then the flames of the fire flickered across the room, warming us—the first fire in days. Flora walked over to Sylvan's computer, touching it.

I can almost see Sylvan there in the light of the fire, his hair gray like mine—on his head and on his face. Later, when I learn words, I know that this was called a beard.

I remember when I first spoke words to him. He had read Ox-Cart Man *to me several times because he knew I loved it.*

"Ox-Cart Man is a poem," I say, my own voice startling me.

Sylvan turns from his computer, beaming. "Yes!"

Tears come to his eyes, and I walk over to lick them.

Sylvan reaches up and takes a small mirror off the wall. He holds it so both of us can look into it.

"*Same hair. Same eyes. We both think in words,*" *says Sylvan.*

I'M THE POET

YOU'RE THE DOG.

WHICH ONE'S THE POET?

WHICH ONE'S THE DOG?

"*That isn't a poem, Teddy.*

"*That's our song.*"

Sylvan makes up a tune for it and sings it to me every so often.

"I'd better call my dad. He's probably out of class because of the storm," said Nickel.

"No phone," I said. "Sylvan didn't like phones."

"No phone?" he repeated.

"No."

"The computer?"

"No. Only for Sylvan's writing. He didn't connect it to the outside world. He only used it for his words. And no television. He has . . . he *had* a device for checking the weather. We can look for that later."

"My parents will be worried," said Nickel.

"I wrote a note," said Flora. "I left it on the front seat so Mama would know we had help."

Nickel stared at Flora.

"You? You wrote a note?"

Flora nodded.

"I can write, you know. I wrote *Were safe* in big letters."

No one spoke.

Flora shrugged.

"I made it up. I think I forgot the apostrophe."

"You *are* safe," I said. "You didn't make that up."

"You did a great thing, Flora," said Nickel. "Maybe Mama won't worry."

"I only did one thing," said Flora. "You saved me. You wrapped me in a blanket. You got me out of the cold car."

Nickel shook his head.

"Teddy saved us."

"Maybe it was *you* who found Teddy," said Flora stubbornly.

"We found each other," I said. "The end."

Flora grinned at me.

A log in the fireplace flamed up. The light bounced off the walls like Sylvan's words when he read out loud.

Flora went over to look at pictures of Sylvan. There was one of him surrounded by students in the house. And one of Sylvan and me, our heads close together.

Flora turned.

"That's you," she said.

"After Sylvan saved me."

Flora turned back to the picture.

"Did someone leave you behind before Sylvan rescued you?"

"Yes."

"Like us," she said, still looking at the picture.

Nickel turned from the fireplace, his face sad.

"She didn't leave us, Flora. She went to get help for us," he said.

"Children tell tiny truths," Sylvan told me once. "Poets try to understand them."

It was Flora who told tiny truths. It was Nickel who found them hard to hear. He didn't want to think of his mother leaving them for a long time in a fierce storm.

A log crackled and sent sparks out past the stone hearth. Nickel swept them back.

It was the way it used to be.

Flora stared at me. Somehow I knew what she was thinking. It would be Flora who would ask the question.

"So where is he?" she asked. "Sylvan?"

Her voice was soft. The question was not unkind. But I couldn't answer. I walked to the window and looked out.

Flora didn't follow me.

CHAPTER THREE

The Way It Used to Be

We found cans of food: Sylvan's favorite, baked beans with molasses, and chicken soup, and crackers. No milk.

"I don't like milk, anyway," said Flora.

The wind picked up suddenly, and the cracking and falling of tree limbs shook the cabin. The lights flickered, and we found an oil lamp in case the power went out.

"You can sleep in Sylvan's bed," I said.

"I want to sleep with you in front of the fire," said Nickel.

"Me, too," said Flora.

We gathered pillows and blankets and Sylvan's old green sleeping bag.

The wind grew stronger. A large thump of a big tree limb fell outside.

The lights went off, then on, then off again.

I lay on the red rug.

Flora slept right away.

After a while Nickel turned and put his

arm around me.

The way it used to be.

In the night I got up once to push up the door lever with my nose and go outside into the wind.

Nickel raised his head.

"Where are you going?"

His voice sounded frightened.

"I'm going to pee," I said.

I heard Flora's sleepy, comforting voice in the dark.

"He's a dog," Flora said softly.

"Oh right," said Nickel. "I keep forgetting that."

I came back to my red rug next to Nickel.

His arm went around me again.

"Sometimes I forget, too," I said to Nickel.

CHAPTER FOUR

Gray Cat Gone Away

I n the morning the wind still howled. The snow was halfway up the windows on either side of the door, and still falling hard.

When I opened the door to go outside, the snow was over my head. I couldn't get through.

Nickel had leaned the snow shovel inside the night before, and he shoveled a path through the drifts for me. I leaped through the snow.

Back inside I shook the snow off on the rug by the door.

"Thank you, Nickel," I said.

His hair was plastered to his head. He looked the same way he had when I'd first found him.

Flora still slept by the fire.

"I found the weather box and listened," he said. "The storm will last for days. No one is allowed on the roads. No phone service. No cell phone service working either."

"The power went on and off all night,"

I said. "We only lost power for hours once that I remember, though."

It is a windy afternoon storm. Sylvan's class of poets sit in a group. There is a fire in the fireplace. I lie on the red rug, listening. The students who want to be poets are eager and fresh, like washed apples. Sylvan and I are the only ones with gray, grizzled hair.

"They know so little about life," Sylvan whispers to me as he puts out plates of cookies and seltzer bottles.

"Maybe they just don't know what they know," I say, making Sylvan smile.

They all pat me. Students are always kind to their teachers' pets Sylvan has told me.

One young man reads a poem about a farmer walking his animal to town.

I sit up. It sounds like Ox-Cart Man. Sylvan nods when he's done reading.

"What do you think, Teddy?" he asks.

The students laugh.

"Shallow and derivative," I say before I realize that I'm talking.

No one but Sylvan hears me, of course.

"It has been written a different way, Dan," says Sylvan. "Go read Ox-Cart Man."

A thin, nervous girl, Ellie, reads a poem about her lost love.

Sylvan taps his foot nervously. I know he hates it.

"Ellie, have you lost a love?" Sylvan asks her

when she's finished reading.

She shakes her head. There are tears in her eyes.

I get up from the red rug and go stand next to Ellie.

Her lips tremble.

"What have you lost?" asks Sylvan. "What are you really talking about in this poem?"

I lean against Ellie, and she puts her arm around me.

"My cat," she whispers.

She is crying full-out now, and I glare at Sylvan. I curl my lip at him.

He looks at me, and his face softens.

"Ellie," says Sylvan softly, "write about your cat, dear girl."

*And the lights go out, Ellie's tears making the
ruff of my neck wet in the dark room.*

*"You were not kind to her," I tell Sylvan
later.*

He sighs.

*"I know. Sometimes writers are not
thoughtful of other writers. We want to be
inspired. Cranky when we're not. But trust me,
she will write a wonderful poem about her cat."*

And she does.

It's called "Gray Cat Gone Away." It ends:

In moonlight

No

SOFT SWEET PAW ON MY CHEEK

No

FUR CURLED UNDER MY CHIN

JUST

A SAD SPACE LEFT BEHIND—

GRAY CAT GONE AWAY.

CHAPTER FIVE

Full of Sorrow, Full of Joy

There was no silence in the cabin, even at night. The wind was like a wild song that pushed away the quiet.

The power had gone off and on, off and on many times.

We cooked up many things from the freezer to be heated in the fireplace later.

We stored the cooked food in coolers outside in the snow.

Today Flora cooked soup on the stove, stirring as she read a book.

"This is you, Teddy," she called to me.

When I walked over to the stove, I saw she was reading a book on Irish wolfhound dogs. A tall dog like me was on the cover.

"You're much better looking, I must say," said Flora.

If I could smile I would have.

"Did you know that your ancestors were warriors?" she said, peering over the book at me.

"So Sylvan told me," I said.

"Your great-grandfather or grandmother may have pulled soldiers off horses with their teeth," said Flora.

"I myself have never done that," I said, making Nickel laugh.

"It says here you have a kindly disposition," said Flora.

"Does it say he's a best friend?" asked Nickel, tossing more wood on the fire.

Flora lowered the book and stirred the soup, tossing in some herbs from a small jar.

"Yes," she announced. "It does. And often the Irish wolfhound loves children and cats."

"I have met a cat or two that I liked," I said.

"We have a cat at home," said Flora.

"Is it a spitter?" I asked.

Flora gave me an insulted look.

"She is not a spitter."

A sudden sweep of wind sent snow against the cabin. Outside a limb fell. We all looked up.

"This is lasting a long time," said Nickel. "The batteries for the weather box are getting low, and I don't know how to charge them. But the storm is expected to last for a few more days."

"Good," said Flora. "I like it here."

"I like it here, too," said Nickel. "As long as there's wood to burn and food to eat."

He paused.

"And as long as Mom and Dad aren't worried."

"Remember, I wrote a note," said Flora.

"There's wood in the shed," I said.

"If we can get there," said Nickel.

"And food in the pantry," said Flora.

"I like it here, too," I said suddenly. "I do."

Sylvan types on his computer, sometimes smiling, sometimes frowning and muttering to himself.

I sit up on the red rug and yawn my yawn that ends with a squeak.

He looks over at me.

"Being a writer is not easy, you know. It is, now that I think of it, either full of sorrow or full of joy."

"Like being a dog," I say.

Sylvan turns in his chair and peers at me.

"I should take my own advice to Ellie and write about what I love."

Sylvan pauses.

"I will write about you."

"The way Ellie wrote about her cat?" I ask.

"Yes," says Sylvan.

He turns back to his computer and writes furiously.

"Ellie is a poet, you know," he says. "At long last. The next time she sees you, she'll hear you speak."

"I know," I say, yawning.

The peal of laughter from Sylvan fills the room. After a moment he laughs more at what he's writing. He coughs a bit at the same time. He has a bottle of medicine and a spoon on his desk. He pours some into the spoon. His cheeks are a little flushed.

After a few minutes he gets up, closes the cover on his computer, and lies down on the couch.

The cough stays with him through the night.

It is the beginning of Sylvan getting sick.

CHAPTER SIX

Something Good

"'Day three in the cabin during a horrific storm,'" Nickel read dramatically from his notebook. "'Flora is rummaging through the refrigerator like a hungry weasel, searching for something mysterious, and possibly poisonous.'"

Nickel wrote silently in his notebook

every day, and had just begun reading his views of our life in the cabin.

His writing is funny, sly, and sometimes poignant. Sylvan had taught me the word *poignant.*

"It may be the most important thing in poetry," Sylvan tells me. "Poignancy."

Sylvan would have said that Nickel had style.

Not once had Nickel asked to use Sylvan's computer. The silver computer sat silently on his desk, cover closed. There was something final about that.

* * *

Sylvan closes his laptop computer with a snap.

"The end. Done-o!"

The loud word **done-o** causes me to leap up from a sound sleep.

Sylvan grins at me and brings a pillow over to my red rug. He lies next to me, one arm around me.

Because I am a dog with a good nose and fine ears, I can hear that he is not breathing easily. He doesn't have the same Sylvan smell that I know.

"You should go to the vet," I tell him.

"The doctor," he corrects me.

"Yes."

"Ellie is driving me to the doctor tomorrow. You can have a nice talk with her."

His grin is huge.

* * *

Flora had become the cook, inventing meals that looked terrible but surprised us by tasting good.

I lap up her soups noisily, the liquid first, then eating whatever she has added at the end.

"That's a much better way to eat soup than with a spoon," said Nickel.

"Peanut butter is very hard," I told him, trying to get it off the roof of my mouth.

"It's not because I'm a girl that I cook," Flora explained. "I like it. It's in the herbs. Like science. When I grow up and have twenty-seven cats and dogs and become a horse trainer, I will have a large collection of herbs."

Nickel laughed, the cheerful sound cutting through the constant noise of the wind outside.

It reminded me of Sylvan's laugh.

"I will find a horse; you just watch," said Flora, turning on the oven.

"And she will," said Nickel.

Nickel and I went outside to the shed while Flora cooked whatever invention she cooked.

It was still hard to get through the wind and drifts. We both ran with our heads down. When we reached the shed, we opened the door and shut it behind us.

The shed smelled the sweet smell of cut wood. It was strangely warm and quiet.

Nickel leaned against the woodpile for a moment.

"This is where you slept after Sylvan left," he said, nodding at the pile of gray blankets behind the woodpile.

"Yes."

"You didn't want to sleep in the house alone."

"No."

"Were you warm enough?"

"Most nights."

Nickel sighed.

"But what will happen to you after Flora and I go home?"

I didn't answer.

After a moment Nickel started loading wood into the log carrier.

Just before we opened the door to fight our way back to the cabin, Nickel turned.

"Something good will happen. I know. After all, you once had Sylvan," he said.

He said it with a poignant tone. That word again.

Poignant.

When we were out in the snow and wind again, walking quickly, Nickel suddenly touched my head.

"Look."

In the clearing close to the woods stood a deer, the color of dawn, watching us.

"A sign of something good," said Nickel.

We hurried on, and when we both looked back, the deer was gone.

CHAPTER SEVEN

Going Away

I told them in the morning. I didn't want to tell them at night. Night could bring dreams.

We were eating pancakes that Flora had made without milk, strange and grainy and wonderful, with lots of maple syrup. I licked the syrup off first, then ate the pancake in small bits.

Nickel watched me and ate his pancake the same way. It made Flora laugh.

Nickel had found the cord to charge the weather box.

"More days of bad weather. Ice is possible before the storm ends. The roads will be cleared after two days. Things will open again. Electricity will be back on in most places."

"So," I said suddenly, "Sylvan got very sick."

I hadn't meant to say it right out like that.

Nickel put down his fork.

Flora opened her mouth, but for the

first time since I'd known her, no words came out.

"You didn't think he'd just gone away and left me, did you?" I asked. "After all I've told you about him?"

Flora shook her head, still silent.

I could see tears at the edges of Nickel's eyes.

"That's the story," I said. "He got sick."

Ellie comes to drive Sylvan to the doctor. The day is sunny, and she walks into the house without knocking.

"Hello, Teddy," she says.

She puts her head down next to mine and hugs me.

"Hello, Ellie," I say.

She grins.

"I can hear you," she says happily.

"You're a poet," I say.

Sylvan comes into the living room dressed in a tweed jacket over a blue shirt.

His eyes are as blue as the shirt.

"Did I hear you two talking?" he asks slyly.

"Yes," says Ellie. "I'm wondering if my dog, Billy, will talk to me when I get home."

"No," says Sylvan, "but don't worry. You'll have many hours to read to him."

Ellie sighs.

"No, Billy is more of a sleeper," she says.

"I'll drive," says Sylvan, who since I've known him has only ridden a bike.

Ellie is no fool.

"Do you have a driver's license?" she asks.

"No, he's a poet," I say, making Ellie laugh.

"I'm driving," says Ellie. "You can sit next to me and roll out your lovely words."

Ellie strokes my head.

"Do you want to ride in the car with us?" she asks me.

"I'll wait here," I say.

I don't want to leave the house. I'm afraid that if I leave, somehow everything may change.

I walk outside and watch them drive off in Ellie's small red car.

Going away.

CHAPTER EIGHT

Curmudgeon

I hear Ellie's car drive up to the front door.

Sylvan told me about the theater once. I feel
like I'm watching a stage play.

Sylvan comes in looking tired.

He takes off his tweed jacket and stretches out
on the couch.

Ellie carries a paper bag.

"That doctor's office made me sick,"
complains Sylvan. "There must be an ocean of
germs there. That's why I don't like going to the
doctor."

"You went there sick," says Ellie.

She takes bottles of medicine out of the paper
bag and sets them by the sink.

She sits on a stool next to Sylvan.

"He wouldn't let me know what the doctor
said," Ellie says to me.

"You are not my mother," says Sylvan, his
arm covering his eyes. "You are much more
beautiful than my mother."

"Thank you," says Ellie.

"He has a fever," I say.

Sylvan takes his arm away from his eyes and stares at me.

"How do you know that?"

"I'm a dog. I smelled a fever, and I can hear chest rumbles in you."

"See?" says Sylvan with more energy. "I don't need a doctor. I have a dog!"

"Take your pills and drink lots of water," says Ellie.

"I don't much like water," says Sylvan.

Ellie laughs a lot.

"I'll be back tomorrow for the class if you're well enough to have it here," she says.

"Only if someone reads a real poem," says Sylvan.

"Curmudgeon," whispers Ellie as she kisses me on the top of my head.

"Rest," she calls as she goes out the door.

Sylvan doesn't rest.

He smiles at me as he sits at the computer.

"I like that girl," he says. "And I heard her call me a curmudgeon," he adds as he types.

"I guess there is nothing wrong with your ears," I say.

"Thank you, Doctor Dog," says Sylvan with sarcasm.

"And you took care of Sylvan," said Nickel.

"I did."

"Like he took care of you," said Flora.

Nickel's voice was soft, but I could hear him even with the storm outside.

"It's almost as if Sylvan saved you and brought you here so you could save us."

"Maybe. One night, late, Sylvan read me part of a poem he had written about me. He called it 'HE the Poet's Dog.'" I closed my eyes to remember it.

> HE THE POET'S DOG
>
> PICKS UP MY DROPPED WORDS
>
> HE
>
> CARRIES THEM IN HIS SOFT MOUTH
>
> LIKE TREASURES
>
> TO BURY
>
> FOR LATER

So

HE THE POET'S DOG

CAN PASS THEM ALONG

AND I CAN FOLLOW.

Flora put her hand on my back.

"All this time I've been mad that Sylvan left you. But maybe he didn't really leave at all.

"At all," she repeated softly.

CHAPTER NINE

Memories

It was an evening with no power—a fireplace fire, oil lamps, a candle on the table.

Nickel wrote in his notebook.

The room was warm, but Flora sat with a blanket around her shoulders. She had a faraway look.

"What are you thinking about?" I asked her.

"My youth," she said.

Nickel grinned.

"Like now?" he asked.

Flora shook her head.

"I feel different."

"You *are* different," I said. "You've been brave. You wrote a note and left it for your mother. You kept us in good food for nearly five days."

I thought of Sylvan's students, romping through life like puppies—young people trying to write their way into adulthood.

"Do you remember when I was born?" Flora asked Nickel.

"I do. I wanted a guinea pig."

"Do you remember when you were young?" Flora asked me.

"I'm not sure my memories are like yours. I remember Sylvan most because he gave me words for my memories. Before that I remember moments, but I had no words for them."

Flora lifted her shoulders and sighed.

"I think I feel different because I have worries. I never had worries before now."

"What are you worried about?" asked Nickel.

"Not what. Who," said Flora.

"Who?" I asked.

Flora stared at me.

"You," she said.

Nickel looked up from his writing, waiting to hear what I'd say.

I worried about me, too. But I didn't want to tell them that.

"I have Ellie," I said. "Don't worry."

Ellie visits us every day. Sometimes she brings food for dinner.

For a while Sylvan seems better. He writes every day. He reads to me every day.

When Sylvan forgets to take his medicine, I shake the bottles in my mouth so he remembers.

The poets arrive for a class, and the boy who

tried to write Ox-Cart Man *in his own words reads a poem Sylvan loves. It's called "The Crazy Cows of Spring."*

THE COWS ARE CRAZY WITH SPRING,

BREAKING THROUGH THE FENCE

GALLOPING TO TOWN

LEAVING THEIR COW PIES

BEHIND.

Flora and Nickel seemed comforted by the idea of Ellie taking care of me every day.

"She can't get here because of the storm," I told them. "But she knows that I can get in the house and find my open bag of dog food in the bottom pantry bin." I paused. "Sylvan taught me that."

It was bedtime, and we laid down blankets and pillows on the red rug.

"And when you're back home, Ellie will drive me to visit you. In her little red car."

"Let's have a party tomorrow to celebrate," said Flora. "I found a can of frosting in the pantry."

A party.

We turned off the oil lamps and blew out the candle. We could hear ice pellets hitting the windows and roof.

The three of us slept in a heap in front of the fire.

All night.

Together.

CHAPTER TEN

....

Silence

We woke in the morning at the same time, raising our heads, listening for the sound of wind.

We heard nothing. We looked at one another.

Silence.

The storm had ended.

Surprisingly, Flora burst into tears.

Nickel sat up and put his arm around her.

"It's all right, Flora," he said. "We knew the storm wouldn't last forever."

"Can we still have a party?" Flora asked.

I left Flora in the pantry, "rummaging" (Nickel's word) for frosting. Nickel scooped out old ashes from the fireplace and built a new fire for the day.

I lifted the door lever and went outside to stand in the quiet. Then I leaped through the deep snow, through the woods, around the pond, and out to the road where Flora and Nickel's car had been. I stood looking down the road. The quiet was almost as loud as the noise of the wind.

The snow was high. No one had plowed. It was the longest stretch of white I'd ever seen—up and down the long road.

I listened, but there were no faraway sounds of cars or plow trucks.

Silence.

I turned and went back around the pond, heavy with snow. I passed trees with branches all white.

Then home.

I shook the snow off my body, then lifted the lever and walked inside.

Flora and Nickel looked at me.

"We can have a party. There's time," I
said.

Ellie comes to take Sylvan back to the doctor.
She brings me snacks.

Sylvan looks tired and weak, though he has
been taking his medicine.

"I plan to talk to the doctor with you today,"
says Ellie.

"Don't be a nag," says Sylvan.

"I have to be a nag. You have Teddy to care
for."

Sylvan looks at her as he opens the front door.

He looks at me then.

"Yes. I do," he says softly.

When they come home again, I can tell they have been arguing.

"You should go to the hospital if the doctor says so," says Ellie.

"Not yet. You get sick in the hospital," says Sylvan.

Ellie lifts her shoulders.

"All right then. I'm leaving you with my cell phone. You can call my landline if you need me. And that's that."

No one speaks. Ellie and Sylvan stare at each other as if at war.

Finally Sylvan gives in.

"All right," he says. "Leave the phone."

And that is when I know Sylvan will not live long.

Ellie gives me a kiss on the head.

As she opens the door, Sylvan calls to her.

"Thank you, Ellie."

I see a flash of tears in her eyes.

Sylvan puts his hand on my head the way he does when we walk in the woods.

Then he goes to his computer with his tweed jacket still on.

He writes something and prints it out.

Then he goes to the couch where he sleeps all night long.

I don't sleep on my red rug, even though a low fire burns there.

I sleep next to where Sylvan sleeps, waking to watch and listen to him.

At dawn he wakes.

He takes Ellie's cell phone out of his pocket. He dials a number.

"Ellie? Please come," he says.

He looks at me.

"Ellie will care for you. But I hope you find a jewel or two, Teddy."

A jewel or two? What does he mean?

I lean against him.

"A jewel or two," he repeats. "Trust me."

And he closes his eyes, his hand still on my neck.

By the time Ellie gets there he is still.

Silence.

Much later Ellie finds Sylvan's printed note on the desk next to his computer. Ellie reads it to me.

"Dear Teddy and Ellie,

You both made my life joyful.

I have left the cabin to Teddy with both your names there and on my bank account. Ellie, I know you will make sure Teddy is fine. And as you offered, you will be Teddy's guardian to help him find a life with someone who hears his wise words.

I love you both.

Sylvan."

Ellie puts her arms around me.

"We will both be fine," she says, her voice quiet and strong.

CHAPTER ELEVEN

The Past and the Present

The party food was chocolate-frosted cookies, hard as stone but tasty.

Flora dribbled frosting on my kibbles. I didn't tell her chocolate was not good for dogs.

I lifted the door lever and went outside. Nickel had shoveled every day, so that I walked out on a snow path to look at all the white.

Suddenly I saw a faraway figure, dressed in red, skiing through the woods. The figure came closer and closer, coming out of the woods into the clearing toward the house.

I knew who it was!

"Teddy!" called Ellie.

I couldn't believe how happy I was to see her. I wagged my tail and jumped on her as she stopped. She laughed and patted me as she took off her skis, falling down in the snow to hug me.

"Teddy," she said, out of breath. "I was worried about you in the storm!"

"Did you ski all the way from home?"

"Yes. It was the only way to get to you. My car is buried, and the snow and ice on the roads aren't cleared."

"I know."

She looked at the chimney of the cabin.

"There's smoke from a fire!"

I got up, and we walked to the cabin door.

"I didn't build it," I said to Ellie. "You'd better come in."

Ellie leaned her skis against the house. We opened the door.

Inside the warm cabin, Nickel and Flora turned from the fireplace. Nickel's eyes widened when he saw another human with me.

"This is Ellie!" I said happily. "This is Ellie."

Nickel and Flora loved Ellie right away. Ellie loved the hard cookies with chocolate frosting. She ate three of them, sitting in front of the fire with her hand on my neck.

"I heard on my radio that you two were saved by a family with six children," said Ellie. "You left a note on the front seat of your mother's car."

We looked at Flora.

Flora actually blushed.

"I forgot that part of the note," she said. "I added a bit."

Ellie laughed.

"It worked. Your parents were not worried about you. Probably tomorrow or the day after, the roads will begin to be cleared. Maybe all the power will be back on."

She paused.

"I'm glad that you came here," she said to Nickel and Flora.

"We're glad Teddy saved us," said Nickel.

"I learned how to save you," I said.

"From Sylvan," said Flora, nodding. "Teddy told us about Sylvan."

All of a sudden Ellie sat up straight, a strange look on her face.

"I just realized something amazing. And wonderful."

"What?" asked Nickel.

Ellie took a deep breath.

"You and Flora hear Teddy's wise words," she said.

She took my face in her hands.

"They do," she whispered. "What Sylvan wished for."

"They do. You do," I said. "A bit like the past and the present coming together, don't you think?"

Ellie grinned.

"I do think!" she said, nodding.

CHAPTER TWELVE

Promises

Ellie made her way home again after lunch, carrying the telephone number of Nickel and Flora's parents.

"Their names are Ruby and Jake," said Nickel. "It's probably best to tell them you were here when Teddy found us. They might not understand us being saved by an

Irish wolfhound."

"I'll tell them you're fine and give them directions to this house," said Ellie. "And I *am* here. They could surprise you, of course. They might be so happy to see you both that they won't care who found you."

"I don't remember them ever surprising me," said Flora.

"Except when they try to dance, don't forget," said Nickel.

Flora nodded.

"They are not very good at dancing," she said thoughtfully.

Outside, Ellie put on her skis again.

She kissed us all and went off, a red spot against the white.

"I'll take you all for a ride in my little red car!" she called back to us, waving.

"Thank you!" called Flora.

We watched her ski off, slowly disappearing into the woods and out of sight.

"She'll be back," said Nickel, watching me.

"She will," I said. "She's Ellie."

Nickel rolled a snowball in his hands and tossed it in the air.

I leaped up and caught it in my mouth.

It had no taste.

That night we ate a very good stew warmed on the grate of the fireplace.

"What's in this?" I asked.

"Never mind," said Flora.

"That means you don't want to know," Nickel said.

I nodded and kept eating.

"I wasn't sure Ellie was real," said Nickel as he ate.

"I knew that," I said.

"I don't mind going home so much now that I've met Ellie," said Flora. "But I'll miss you, Teddy," she added.

My throat felt tight.

"Just remember the red car," I said finally.

"You promise a visit?" she said.

"I promise, I promise, promise, promise, promise . . . ," I said.

Flora and Nickel laughed.

I knew they would. I knew they believed
me.

And we slept for the last time together—

In a heap—

In front of the fireplace—

In the quiet cabin.

CHAPTER THIRTEEN

A Jewel or Two

It happened before we thought it would.

The knock at the door—

Nickel opening the door—

A man I knew must be his father
sweeping Nickel up in his arms—

Nickel crying.

I'd never seen Nickel cry until now,

only the tear streaks on his face the day I found him in the storm.

Flora stood by the fireplace, watching. I went to stand next to her, and she put her hand on my neck the way I love.

Nickel's father looked over at Flora then. He came into the house, closing the door behind him.

"Thank you for your note, Flora," he said, coming over to take her hand. I don't think he even noticed me beside her. He picked her up and hugged her. She put her arms around his neck.

I liked the smell of him.

"Ellie told me that she had been here with you," her father said.

Flora leaned back, and her father put her down.

"This is Teddy," she said. "*He* found us. *He* saved us and brought us here, not the family with six children. I made them up so you wouldn't worry."

Her father stared at me for a moment.

"Hello, Teddy, I'm Jake," he said.

"Hello, Jake," I said.

Jake shook his head a bit, looking confused.

"He doesn't hear your words," whispered Flora very softly.

"I know. I am used to answering questions whether people hear me or not. But he hears *something*."

Jake looked over my head at the book-shelf.

"Wait," he said. "Who lives here? Was this Sylvan's house? I see his pictures on the wall. I see his books on the shelf."

We were surprised.

"Yes," said Nickel. "Sylvan lived here with Teddy. He rescued Teddy the way Teddy rescued us."

Jake sat down.

"You're the Teddy of his poem 'HE the Poet's Dog,'" he said softly.

"Yes," I said.

Jake bent his head as if listening to something far away.

Flora smiled a little.

"He was my teacher," said Jake. "And he sent me the poem."

Jake grinned.

"Sylvan told me once that I could be a poet if I wasn't so lazy."

Nickel laughed.

Flora went over to her father.

"I'm not going home without Teddy," she said.

There was a big silence in the cabin.

I felt the hair on my neck stand up a bit.

Finally Jake shrugged his shoulders.

"You're right, Flora Jewel. If Teddy saved you, he should come home with us. He doesn't have Sylvan now," he added.

Jewel?

Flora noticed my startled look.

"It's my middle name," she whispered. "Silly. My mother is Ruby."

Not silly. Not silly at all.

"Will you come home with us, Teddy?" asked Flora.

I thought of leaving my cabin. How could I do that?

Flora saw my face.

Flora always seemed to know what I was thinking.

"Ellie can bring you back here for visits. Whenever you want."

"Yes, he will come home," Nickel said.

Jake stroked my head.

"Yes, he will come home with us," he said.

Flora Jewel?

We put out the fire and closed the cabin door. We walked up the hill where Jake's big car was parked.

I don't remember ever being in a car before. Surely Sylvan brought me home from the shelter in someone's car.

But that was when I didn't have words.

Nickel leaned over close to me in the backseat.

"I think he almost hears you speak," he whispered. "He isn't a poet, but he wouldn't mind being one. He teaches literature."

"*You* can hear me. That's what really matters," I said. "And you never told me he teaches literature."

"You didn't ask me," Nickel said.

Jake called Ruby on his cell phone on our ride home.

"Ruby? I have Flora and Nickel. We're on our way home. They were rescued by a wonderful dog. Teddy took them to his home and cared for them. Ruby? Teddy is coming home with us, too."

There was silence as Jake listened. He looked at us in the rearview mirror and smiled.

"Ruby says great!"

And we rode home on snowy roads, past

snow-covered meadows and ponds and trees.

The whole way there we were the only car.

The only car in the whole world.

When we got to the big white house on the hill and got out of the car, the front door opened, and Ruby ran into the cold without her coat.

Flora and Nickel ran up the hill to hug her.

And then she saw me. She burst into tears, reminding me of Flora.

"An Irish wolfhound! You didn't tell me he was an Irish wolfhound! I grew up with one all of my childhood."

She put her hand on my neck and knelt down with her face next to mine like Flora did when I first took her to the cabin in the snowstorm.

"Jewel was the best dog in the world, and you look just like her!"

Jewel.

Ruby put her hand on my neck.

"Welcome home, Teddy," she said.

"Find a jewel or two," Sylvan had said. "Trust me."

And as we walked up the hill, I felt Sylvan was walking alongside me.

Flora was right.

Sylvan had never left at all.